This orchard
book belongs to

....

....

For Mattie and Bill

www.alisonmurray.net

ORCHARD BOOKS
338 Euston Road, London NW1 3BH
Orchard Books Australia
Level 17/207 Kent Street, Sydney, NSW 2000

First published in 2012 by Orchard Books
First published in paperback in 2013

ISBN 978 1 40831 199 8

Text and illustrations © Alison Murray 2012

2 4 6 8 10 9 7 5 3 1

A CIP catalogue record for this book is available from the British Library.

Printed in China

Orchard Books is a division of Hachette Children's Books, an Hachette UK company.
www.hachette.co.uk

Hickory Dickory
DOG

Alison Murray

ORCHARD

Hickory, dickory, dock,
A dog, a boy . . .

. . . a clock!

The day's begun,

It's time for fun!

Hickory, dickory, dock.

Hickory, dickory, dear, Rufus has to stay here.

There's a whine and a pine,

And a wet paint sign. Hickory, dickory, dear.

Hickory, dickory, dare,

NO DOGS
ALLOWED

Dogs aren't allowed in there.
A sneaky peek through . . .

Then a **hullabaloo!**

Hickory, dickory, dare.

Hickory, dickory, dee,

Haroo!

Hurrah!

Yippee!

The clock strikes eleven,

It's make-a-mess heaven!

Hickory, dickory, dee.

Hickory, lickery, lunch.
Some yummy crumbs to munch.

The clock strikes noon,

Zac's dropped his spoon!

Hickory, lickery, lunch.

Hickory, dickory, doo.
Uh-oh! A gloop of glue!

The weather is fine . . .

...so it's garden time.

Hickory, dickory, doo.

Hickory, stickory, stack.
A scritchety, scratchety back.

Time is up, you mucky pup!
Hickory, stickory, stack.

Higglety, pigglety, pup.
It's home to clean you up!

The clock strikes five.

Slip,

Slide,

Crash . . .

. . . Dive!

Higglety, pigglety, pup.

Hickory, flickory, fly. Rufus still needs to get dry.

First a bit of an itch.

Then a twist and a twitch.

Hickory, flickory, fly.

Hickory, dickory, dock.

A dog, a boy, a clock.

Now, it's time
For the end of the rhyme . . .

Hickory, dickory, dog.